Step Inside

Edited by Marcia Coppess.

Design and Illustration by Karen Newe.

WinePress Publishing (P.O. Box 428, Enumclaw, WA 98022) functions only as book publisher. As such, the ultimate design, content, editorial accuracy, and views expressed or implied in this work are those of the author.

The following stories have been published previously in other form:

Step Inside © 1982 by Melea J. Brock
The King Who Waits © 1982 by Melea J. Brock
The Sack © 1994 by Melea J. Brock
The Land of Stinky Feet © 1993 by Melea J. Brock
The Worriers © 1995 by Melea J. Brock
The Fountain © 1986 by Melea J. Brock
The Regular Kingdom and the Beautiful Kingdom © 1982 by Melea J. Brock
Suitcases © 2002 by Melea J. Brock
The Grudge Bearer © 2002 by Melea J. Brock
A Song for the Darkness © 2006 by Melea J. Brock
The Giants Without Manners © 2005 by Melea J. Brock
The Land of Sighs © 2003 by Melea J. Brock
The Great King's Longing © 2005 by Melea J. Brock

Scripture quoted in The Worriers is from *The Message* © 1993 by Eugene H. Petersen used by permission of the NavPress Publishing Group.

The Doxology, 1560, public domain.

ISBN 13: 978-1-57921-851-5
ISBN 10: 1-57921-851-2
Library of Congress Catalog Card Number: 2006900971

Printed in China.

APC-FT5336

Step Inside

Where Stories
Come to *Life*

❦ CD Included ❧

MELEA J. BROCK

WINEPRESS WP PUBLISHING *and*

If we are all caught in *the story* then there must be a Storyteller.

And if there is a *Storyteller* then your part and my part in this story must

truly matter to Him . . . .

And so, this book is dedicated to the Storyteller

and all His beloved children.

Special Acknowledgments

No great effort is ever accomplished without the help of others. I am a rich person for the help I have received in this project of *Step Inside . . . Where Stories Come to Life*. My applause and deepest thanks go to these individuals:

- David, my wonderful husband, and Timothy & Gracie, my dear children.
- Marcia Coppess, my enduring and endearing editor.
- Karen Newe, my incredible graphic artist of many years.
- Gary and Cindy Bayer, my prayer partners and family.
- Perry Moore, my brother, composer and hilarious co-creator of this CD.
- David Buller for the CD "producership" and help with our Right-Side-Up Stories Studio.
- Athena Dean, Tim Noreen, and the staff at WinePress for their creativity and patience with this particular writer and storyteller.

- Pastor Jack Hayford and Pastor Jim Tolle for their affirmation of my gifts and sound shepherding of my soul and spirit.

- Ray Rood, my mentor and friend, who believes that knowing one's story is of ultimate value to the world, maybe even the Universe!

- My writing companion, Cari Beck-Taylor, who has encouraged me to write and love the process. All the salad, coffee, and honest conversation has meant so much to this work and all the other ones we *will* write.

- Our Home Group at The Church On The Way for their prayers

- "The Sisters"—there was a choir of women *singing away* during the last year and a half of this book's creation. Their singing came in the form of prayers, cards, e-mails, childcare, sweet counsel, and support. Thank you Ann Marie Batesole, Charisse Bell, Rebecca Best, Deborah Boyle, Maureen Broderson, Ceci Carroll, Theresa Chesshir, Lorraine Coconato, Margie Coffin, Tess Cox, Jen Crawford, Prudence and Shaleah Dancy, Vicky Eagleson, Kelly Frey, Bea Grushow, Reneé Herman, Mercy Ising, Ginger Luber, Linda Rand, Angie Settlemire, Andrea Tolle, Joyce Vasquez, Susie Williams, and Jessica Zachman.

To you, my readers, thank you for taking the time to read and use these stories. My hope is that your story has been restored between some of these pages.

Everyone hopes for the applause of others in a project, but the applause that would mean the most to me would be that from the nail-scarred hands of the Storyteller. My own applause goes to the Father and His Son. Thank you for allowing me the privilege of creating another book that bears my name and your Truth. And to the precious gentle Holy Spirit, thank you for your guidance and creativity.

Contents

Step Inside

There's something about a story for me.

A special invitation to come away.

Shhh . . . be quiet.

Crawl upon a lap.

It's as if the world stops spinning 'round,

And the day's troubles take a nap.

And I make the choice to listen

To the secret something bound and wound

In lines and pictures there.

Oh, yes!

There is something about a story,

If I allow its words to woo,

To tickle, tease, poke, and

prod the Me within the Who.

"The Who?" you ask.

Well, it's the Who I think I am.

The Who I long to be,

The Who that's hidden

way down deep,

The Who that's really Me.

So step inside
this place with me,
It's ours for just a blink.
A place for me and you to sit,
to feel, to think.

Perhaps, somewhere
within a story,
We'll take a step or two,
Look back and see
our footprints—
Our Me within the Who!

An Introduction

Look back and see our footprints—Our Me within the Who!

I've always loved the ending line of this little poem. Footprints. Footprints are the evidence of a distance traveled. And as I anticipate your time spent between the pages of this book and your own stepping inside the stories, I am certain you will discover things about the *who* you think you are, the *who* you long to be, the *who* that's hidden way down deep, and that incredible, altogether wonderful *who* that is really and truly you. There will be footprints.

This collection represents some of my best work as a storyteller and writer. Some stories are time-worn as I've told them hundreds of times. Some are new, and their life and value to me, the teller, and you, the listener, has just begun. In the back cover of the book you'll find a compact disk of the six new stories. I hope you will enjoy what happens when I tell you a story. I know I had a ton of fun creating it for you.

In between the stories, I share my thoughts about the rich value of story. Let's think of it as our little coffee break. We'll step away from the right brain activity of these stories and pick up that beautiful left side of our brain. I want to provide you with more than a collection of stories; my hope is that this book will encourage you to explore your own story and use of stories.

Besides enjoying my stories on the page and in CD, please take the time to tell them to others. It's such a brave thing to do—to lift a story with your voice. And if you'd like to bring any of my stories to a public performance level, I've provided some simple guidelines here in the book.

Most authors hope their books linger on coffee tables or bookshelves or are passed on to readers' friends or family members. My hope is that my book does more than that. I want these stories to linger in your heart and mind and soul. I want them to come to life in you. So step inside with me . . . .

Enjoy! Melea

THE King

WHO

Waits

My first oral story—

written to encourage college students

in their search for a personal

and intimate relationship with God.

May it do the same for you.

There is a King, unlike any other king you've read about in history books or fairy tales. A king far too wonderful ever to be compared to any of these kinds of kings. For this one Great King does not merely seek power or rule, but relationship with His subjects. All subjects who seek Him earnestly become heirs to all the great and wonderful treasures the King has been storing away for them since the beginning of time.

By now, you might be wondering, "What does this King want in return for all of that?" I have stumbled through my life over that very question. Stumbled and stumbled. But last night I learned the answer. All this Great King wants in return is just that we come.

Every day the Great King, long before His subjects have risen, begins a morning ritual of preparation. He thrusts open all the windows to let in the scents of early morning, washes the marble entryway, waxing and polishing it to a brilliant shine. He prepare the meals for the day, cuts fresh flowers and places them in all the rooms, and carefully inspects the library to be sure that all is ready for Him and His subjects.

The library is my favorite room in the King's mansion, and I believe that if He had to choose one room, this would be His favorite too. It holds a special place for many reasons—the pictures of His subjects that line the piano, the trinkets many have given Him, scattered here and there, the huge stone fireplace with its two worn but comfortable overstuffed chairs. Three of the four walls are lined with books from floor to ceiling. The fourth has an enormous picture window complete with dreamy landscape. It's the kind of room you'd want to spend the day in—willingly, gladly.

Maybe that's why the Great King is always there when I come. He's always there, sitting in one of the overstuffed chairs. And never has a day passed when He hasn't offered me a brownie, a raspberry tart, or even a meal in His beautifully tiled kitchen. There seems to be no end to His care and concern for me. Such a loving King!

Yet I can't remember the last time I stayed longer than 10 or 15 minutes or met His greeting with the same warmth as He showed me.

You see, I am one of His subjects who has always kept Him waiting—and wondering whether I'd ever show up at all. I'm always in a hurry. But not today. Last night changed my reason for going forever.

You see, last night I dropped by for only a few minutes. I told the Great King, "I've been running around for everyone else today, and tonight, dear King, it's time for me." As I was babbling on, I noticed the King drawing away. He began to share about His day. The King had never done this before. He said He had cleaned, prepared everything, and finally sat back in one of the overstuffed chairs, ready for the first subjects who would be dropping by before work, school, and the busyness of life. "Hour upon hour passed," He said. "And no one came by."

He forgave them, just the same, and continued to wait and wait and wait. And as He waited, He began to daydream about His subjects—when they first met Him, how they'd grown, all their special times together. He said He had thought of me that day. Of course, I was very touched. He said he had remembered, among all our times together, this past spring. How depressed and alone I'd felt. His smiling eyes affirmed my memory.

"Remember?" He said. "We spent the day together." I assured the Great King that I did remember that day. I remember that I left His mansion feeling better than I had felt in months.

His eyes were different now. "I waited for you." His words were not condemning me. "I waited for you to return and tell me things were better. I waited weeks without a word from you."

Well, I was beginning to feel that gnawing, almost sick-to-the-stomach feeling. The kind that comes when a dear friend confronts me about a hurt I've caused.

He continued His story. The striking of noon had brought the King back to the present, and still no one had come. Once again, the Great King forgave and headed off to the kitchen to prepare the noon meal. "One of the loneliest sandwiches I'd eaten in a long time," He added.

He was clearing the extra sandwiches away and brushing the crumbs from His place when an overwhelming sadness swept over Him. He dropped to the cold floor and began to weep. "I want them. I want them. Oh, how I want them. When will they understand?"

After a bit, the Great King pulled Himself up from that cold floor, patted dry the tears, and brushed off His robes, and went back to the library to wait for the first subject.

It was me. I was that first subject. And as He opened the doors, I didn't notice the tear-stained cheeks or the hands outstretched to embrace me as never before. I hadn't noticed any of that. In fact, it wasn't until I sat down with Him face to face at that small, wooden table and heard those words,

"I want them." My Great King served me one more meal and again said, "I simply want them." It wasn't until then that I realized—the Great King wants me! The Great King wants *me*!

Oh, please hear this: the Great King of the Universe and the entire expanse beyond it wants me, and He wants you.

We talked and talked late into the night. We had sandwiches, brownies, and raspberry tarts far too late, but we had the best time I remember spending in all our times together. It was very late when I left His mansion. But that night I took a step closer to Him. A step I could have taken long ago in my life. A step I never had time for until yesterday.

And today will be different. Today, I will spend time with my King. Today I will give more than I think I can spare. And today I'm going to listen, instead of always asking and wanting and talking. He has so much to offer me. He has so much to offer you. The Great King who waits has waited long enough for this subject. ⟡

We Were Made for Story

God so wants us to live in the larger story—His Story.

But the choice is ours . . .

Life began as a story. Go to the first chapter of Genesis in the Bible and you will find a strong narrative, compelling dialogue, and clear descriptions there. God, the greatest storyteller and artist extraordinaire, spoke His creation into being. The comment at the end of this first chapter in His story is this: "And God saw that it was good."

In fact, God's Story has an incredible beginning and a magnificent ending. You and I are living somewhere in the middle of this story. Not the easiest place to live at times—in the middle of a story. Life can get so loud that we can barely hear one another, let alone God. Yet He keeps speaking. The narrative, dialogue, and description He pursues with us daily is that of an Author deeply devoted to His work. Oh, how He loves us.

He speaks to us in the beauty of a sunrise; the small, brown sparrow seeking its food on a snowy road; a child's infectious laughter; or an old and wrinkled face brightened by the remembrance of a moment once lived. He speaks to us in mundane and ordinary things while we're driving to a destination; running an errand; enduring a dry lecture in a classroom; or preparing a meal while juggling a fussy baby. And God is never the silent One at a funeral, graduation, wedding, birthday celebration, or other milestone in our lives, is He?

He speaks.

So if God is doing all this talking, all this storytelling, what's going on in me and you that is stopping that flow? Why are we missing out on His communication? Why can't we hear Him?

I believe I know part of the answer. We need to have our stories restored to us. We restore furniture, books, photos, paintings, cars, houses, land, water—even our hair. What if there was a way to restore what is eroded away by our culture, the stuff of life, sin, and self? What if there was something you and I could do to restore our stories?

There is. It's all about story. If I had the way or means, I would pass out a prescription for all people that would read something like this:

Take one restoring story per day. Results are best when consumed in large quantities and shared in community.

Jesus used a prescription like this. Wherever and whenever He spent time with His creation, He told stories. They were stories that encouraged, enlightened, convicted, taught, and pursued the listeners. They were stories that restored persons. Jesus reached into their lives with a strong narrative, dialogue, and description, and He re-storied them!

My Story with Story

Long ago, while serving as an assistant dean at a small Christian college, I began my work as a storyteller and stepped into, unknowingly, the restorative power of a story.

With my first oral story, "The King Who Waits," in hand, I walked from my office to the residence hall, where students had already gathered for their weekly late, late evening time of community devotions.

My assignment had been given to me by the students: address the issue of having a personal, everyday relationship with God. Instead of lecturing, I decided long before that night to teach these students with a story that I would write for them that very moment. I also decided to make it active and in first person. Therefore, I was the one discovering the change in my own life. I was not talking at the students but inviting them into my own story with God.

I remember those wonderful young adults sitting so still and quiet, like little children captured by a faithful parent in a storytelling moment. I felt empathy from my listeners as I shared my failures and my desire to have an intimate relationship with God once again. There was little need to wrap up with, "OK, here's what I was really trying to say to you." I think I did something the students expected: I prayed. But for the most part, I let the story do its own work. I simply let it fall upon my listeners' ears, knowing that God had things to say to them that evening, just as He had said many things to me while I had written the piece.

Even before I said my final goodbyes, the story began to do its restoration. I can only explain it as a transformation, a righting of heart and mind and soul and spirit. Small confessions and promises were made, and appointments were calendared for further dialogue about what the story had brought to the surface. As the weeks progressed, I realized the shelf life of a simple story. And by shelf life I mean that listeners recalled this story, as with any story, days and weeks later.

One particularly stunning shelf life moment happened weeks later when a young student told me how her life had been changed by hearing "The King Who Waits." As we stood in line to go into the cafeteria, she told me that she now spent time with the Great King. Pointing to a beautiful tree across the campus from us, she said, "He's always there waiting for me, just like you said, Melea."

That day I truly began to understand what it means to restore one's story. I began a journey of partnering with God in His magnificent, out loud, and on purpose storytelling.

You and I—we were made for story.

A Song for the Darkness

❧

O my soul,

bless God!

*C*onstance. It's a good name, a strong name. Constance.

"Constance, you're so like your name," people would tell her.

"Yes, I know. I'm steadfast in purpose and faithful in affection. I'm loyal, unchanging, plodding on . . . just like my birthdays."

Constance had just turned 30, which meant a big party with 30 candles, 30 balloons, 30 presents, 30 friends and family, and 30 days of wondering why she was 30 and unmarried, unsettled in her career, and uninterested in life. She had spent most of the last month of her 29 years complaining about this momentous turning of age.

You've heard of "Forty Days of Purpose"? Well, this was more like "Thirty Days of Pouting."

The great and grand momentous day had come and gone, and now she was living in 30, feeling its weight and a strange, unsettling grief.

"Well, Aunt Lily turned 30 and didn't die," she mused. "Oh, but she did die."

Aunt Lily had passed away some 30 days ago, missing Constance's 30th birthday. She'd been in hospice care for a long time and had finally slipped from here to The Great There.

"Don't weep for me when I'm gone from here, because I'll be There with Him," she'd said.

So perhaps it was Aunt Lily's death that had started Constance pondering (pouting), and not the passing of this third decade. Or perhaps it was all the sorting and sifting through the room on the third floor of Aunt Lily's home.

On weekends since her Aunt's passing, Constance had traveled to the old, empty home, climbed the stairs, and walked into that special room, hoping for a message in the darkness and the dust.

Aunt Lily was what some would probably call "an odd one." She'd never married, but lived in a beautiful, old house and rented rooms to "practically strangers"—that's what Constance's mother called them.

"They're practically strangers, paying practically nothing to you, Lily," she would say, thinking it would change her mind about her renters.

"Ah, but they are God's creatures, made by His own hands," Lily would reply with a smile.

Aunt Lily loved people, God, and her dogs. It was that simple.

And Aunt Lily loved Constance. So much so that Constance was bequeathed Aunt Lily's "upstairs basement," as it was affectionately called. It was a large room filled with the treasures of the world . . . Aunt Lily's treasures.

"This is from the upstairs basement," Aunt Lily would say as she passed you a gift. Or she would write that phrase neatly on the tag of your gift. It was always some unique item that you had never thought of buying for yourself. A little bit of the "upstairs basement" was now a part of your life forever.

Aunt Lily had created this special room and filled it with trinkets, furniture, pictures, photographs, phonograph records, vintage clothing, shoes, hats and accessories, thousands of magazines and books, and far too many things that others would say were ripe for a yard sale or the Goodwill bin.

She also had a peculiar filing system for the room—one that would've amazed the most fastidious of organizers. The markings on the many boxes stacked one upon the other always brought a smile or a chuckle to Constance. Some of her favorites, already sorted through, had been

Joy, Laughter, Unwanted Things, Broken Things, Journals, Love Letters, Dashed Dreams, Dried Flowers from Old Lovers, Recipes for Bad Cooks, Books I am Not Going To Read, and Things Found on the Ground.

Constance pulled another box down and began to sort through its contents. It was a box neatly marked with the word *Hope*.

"Aunt Lily, I hope that's what you found—and I *hope* it's in here."

She opened the box, which held another box. It was a beautiful humidor. Aunt Lily didn't smoke cigars, but she certainly loved the containers they came in.

Constance opened the humidor and found a shiny gold envelope—the only thing inside the box. Inscribed on the outside of the envelope was:

Read in time of need, sing in time of want.
Inside you'll find the answer to all you've ever sought.

For a good 30 minutes, Constance thought about opening the envelope. She carried it downstairs and brewed a strong cup of coffee while waiting for some divine direction from somewhere about what to do with this curious item from the upstairs basement.

She had laid the envelope down on the counter in that just-right place where the midmorning sun poured into the kitchen, a wonderful place to stand on a cold day. The goldenness of the envelope seemed to dance with the sunlight that splashed on the counter. It was kind of hypnotizing as she stared and sipped the coffee.

"Aren't you going to open it, Constance?" said a strong, yet kind voice.

Constance quickly turned around. The voice that spoke those words seemed so audible and clear that she was certain someone had walked into the room and spoken them.

"Great. Now I'm hearing things. I thought this didn't start until your 80's."

She sipped her cup of coffee, feeling the chill of the old house, unnerved by what she thought she had heard from out of nowhere.

"Well, it's back to the upstairs basement, I guess." Constance picked up the envelope, felt its warmth from the sun, and headed back to the room.

Because the kitchen and this room were on the same side of the house, the same sunlight now poured in and lit a small table that she had cleared earlier. On it sat the humidor box, open and empty. Constance walked over and examined the box, looking for a clue—and permission to open the envelope.

"After all," she thought, "this might be someone else's box, someone else's treasured last words from Aunt Lily."

The box was a beautiful green with a metal name plate on the top. The plate was caked with dust, which she rubbed off with a small oilcloth. What was revealed on that name plate took her breath away. It read—*A Song for the Darkness*.

Again the same voice beckoned her, "Open it, Constance."

Her heart started to pound, and tears came to her eyes. The envelope became blurry in her hands as she carefully opened the back flap bit by bit, not wanting to tear it. This was the closest thing to a final word from Aunt Lily that she'd found.

She pulled out a single piece of parchment. It was a piece of music written in perfect notation and script . . .

Praise God, from Whom all blessings flow;

Praise Him, all creatures here below;

Praise Him above, ye heavenly hosts;

Praise Father, Son, and Holy Ghost.

In her head, she could hear the music of a long ago organ filling the room. The Doxology was a familiar song to Constance. One she hadn't thought about or heard in years, though.

At the top of this sheet of music Aunt Lily had written a note to the recipient:

"This song will become your salve for life. It's been my Love Song for the Darkness.

Love always, Aunt Lily"

It had never occurred to Constance that Aunt Lily had had one blue or difficult day in her life. She exuded joy, gratefulness to be alive, and compassion that exceeded that of your basic holy person.

The coolness of the room from the cracked windows hit Constance in the back. She placed the letter on the table and quickly grabbed one of Aunt Lily's fur coats. She then grabbed a pair of gloves and a fancy woolen beret from the neat little piles she had made. She studied herself in the dressing mirror:

"Aunt Lily, you were a classy dresser. You were one incredible woman."

"And so are you," said the Voice.

This was the third time she'd heard this conversational Voice. She stood there staring into the mirror and asked the Voice a question in a demanding tone.

"Is that you, God?"

At that moment, a breeze through the windows blew the piece of music off the table and to Constance's feet. She picked it up with trembling hands, knowing this was not a coincidence but a conversation.

"It *is* you, God. I haven't talked to you in a long time. I'm sorry for that. I've been pretty wrapped up in myself these days . . . well, years. Part of it is that I don't know where I'm headed or what I'm doing with my life. And part of it is that I want someone to share my life with. But where is he, God?"

It was sweet and personal confession.

"So, God, what do want from me? You and Aunt Lily certainly have my attention. I'm listening. I'm really listening this time."

"Sing to Me," said the Voice.

"Sing to You?" she echoed. "I'm no singer, God. I feel like a little kid at a try-out for the school play."

"Sing to Me."

His Voice sounded warm with affection and invitation. In the darkness and dust of years of living, a song of gratefulness rose from a place down deep inside of Constance.

Praise God, from Whom all blessings flow;

Praise Him, all creatures here below;

Praise Him above, ye heavenly hosts;

Praise Father, Son, and Holy Ghost.

With tears flowing freely down her cheeks, she sang the final word as loudly as she could muster: "A-men!"

Constance stood there in the middle of the upstairs basement, magnificently clothed in her Aunt's fur coat, silk gloves, and beret. She held hope in her hands—the Hope that had guided Aunt Lily all her life. The Hope that had never disappointed her. The dressing mirror reflected back to her a woman unchanging, constant, and yet becoming.

"Thank you, Aunt Lily. This love song really works!" ✤

THE *WORRIERS*

This is fun and very honest.

Come on, we all worry.

Take a deep breath

and hold onto your

W's as you tell!

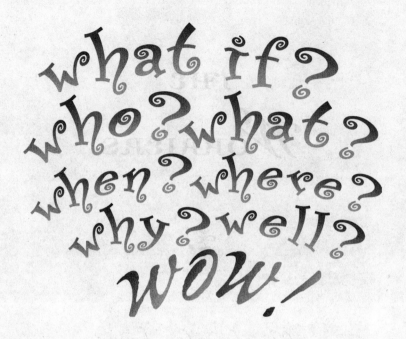

There once was a family, a family of five—Walter, Wilda, Walt Jr., Winnie, and little Willie Worry. And oh, how they did! Worry, that is. They had a nice home, nice neighbors, nice jobs, and nice schools, but they never really knew it, because Walter, Wilda, Walt Jr., Winnie, and little Willie Worry were too busy worrying. They were wearisome worriers. Why they could out-worry the best of 'em. In fact, Walter and Wilda came from a long line of worriers. Both their moms' moms and their dads' dads were worriers and rather proud of it. For you see, when you worry you don't make too many mistakes. You're pretty wary of everyone and everything. Wow, could they worry!

They worried about waking up on time. Upon awakening, they then worried about the weather. And because of the weather worrying, they wondered when to wash and wax the car and when to wash the windows, because one never knows when the weather's going to take a turn for the worse.

They worried about what they ate and whether what they ate would make them gain weight or wane and waste away.

They worried about the way-out economy and the rising cost of wax paper, Necco Wafers, windshield wipers, and bottled water. And was it really wise to have your wisdom teeth pulled?

And sometimes, but not often, they worried about the world and whether people in this world would ever grow weary of having their own way. Now, that's pretty noble worrying, if you ask me.

They worried about their neighbors next door—the Websters and their teenage son, Wesley. Walt Jr. and Wesley were good friends. They were in Mr. Witgenstein's World Civ class and planned to go to West Woonsocket Tech and study word-processing, where upon graduation they would probably wed two winsome women (one each, of course), buy Wedgwood china, work out at the gym, and wait for the big break. But wait, I'm wandering—back to the Websters.

You see, the Websters sometimes took trips on weekends to visit Grandma Webster who was ill, but still very wiry.

The Worrys worried about Wesley on those weekends. They worried about the cars that came to the Webster's with wiggly, giggly teenagers. And well, why would any parent leave a wahoo kind of teenager all alone to weigh and make weighty decisions? What would he eat? When would he go to bed? Where was he going with all of those friends?

On those weekends when the Websters were away, the Worrys got in a whole week's worth of worrying. They were worn out by Wonday, I mean Monday. But still they felt it was worth the worry because they really cared about Wesley and the Websters.

The Websters were the least of their worries when you added them all up though. There were the three different schools their children attended, which averaged several hours of worrying per day. You see, they worried about the education Walt Jr., Winnie, and little Willie were receiving. They wondered about the teachers wearing pants—Miss Williams and Mrs. Watson, that is. And would the wearing of pants by Miss Williams and Mrs. Watson affect their children's education?

They wondered about Coach Weston and why wasn't he warried, I mean married. After all, he was 33! Yes, he seemed very warm and had a winning way with the Walhabi Walrus Water Polo Team, but what was he waiting for—the perfect woman?

They worried about little things like wasting paper in the classrooms, the wax coating on the milk cartons, watering the football field after the weather had taken a turn for the worse, and whether saving the whatchamacallits from the tops of soda cans would really save the whooping crane from extinction.

They worried and they whined to one another, but they never really wanted to get involved. After all, they weren't sure whether they should make waves about these worrisome issues. Surely some other wonderful parent had worried over these very things and made someone aware. And if not, oh well. One can only do so much worrying.

They worried about their jobs and worker's compensation, withholding taxes and the soap in the washroom.

They worried about their church and why there weren't more workers willing to walk the walk *they* walked.

They worried about the city they lived in, Walhabi, Washington, and whether they'd ever have a Dairy Queen like the one in Wenatchee, Washington. The one in Wenatchee used real water-processed decaffeinated coffee and real whipped cream in their Blizzard shakes.

They worried about the reputation of the great apple state of Washington. You see, they could never ever seem to find those little

Winesap apples in the winter. Why? Winesaps were supposed to be available in the winter.

They worried about the United States and warm weather trends from the Mount St. Helen's eruption in 1980. And they worried about preserving the wildlife of these United States such as wild rice, wild oats, wild pansies, wild parsnips, the wild rose, and the infamous game of wild pitch baseball.

Their worry even stretched world wide—to the World Wide Web, of course. And the Windsor Castle in England and the Windsor Family and the Windsor chair, the Windsor knot, the Windsor tie, and were there more Windsor *somethings* in this world to worry about besides all the Windsors they already knew about?

And then one day while the Worrys were sitting on their Windsor chairs, having waffles and going over the worries of the day, the phone rang. It was God. Wow!

Oh yes, God knew the Worrys. He loved the Worrys. He wanted something wonderful for the Worrys. You see, He had tried waking them. He had tried whispering to them. He had tried warning them. He had tried whacking them once. Why God had even tried the wire service. God had something to say to the Worrys.

It was going to startle their stingies, flap their unflappables, wham their worries. The potential was promising. The possibility for monumental and momentous discovery was waiting to be welcomed by the Worrys.

Well, it was Wilda Worry who picked up the phone that day.

"God? As in God the Father?" Her voice quivered with worry as she listened.

"Yes, Walt Sr. is right here eating his waffles. Yes, Walt Jr., Winnie, and little Willie are here too. Put them on the extensions? Right away, God."

Wilda turned to her family, whose jaws had dropped wide open, and said, "Grab a phone! It's God!"

They didn't walk. They all ran to the nearest phone and waited and wondered and worried about what God was going to say.

"Yes, God, we're all here," said Walt Sr.

"Worrys, I want to say something to you. I've been trying to say it to you for a long time." His voice sounded warm, not wild with wrath.

"Yes, God, what is it?" their voices waned a bit.

"My beloved Worrys, are you tired? Worn out? Burned out?"

"Yes," they all said, even little Willie.

"Then come to Me. Get away with Me, and you'll recover your life. I'll show you how to take a real rest. Walk with Me and work with Me. Watch how I do it. Learn the unforced rhythms of my Grace. I won't lay anything heavy or ill-fitting on you. You keep company with me, my beloved Worrys, and you'll learn to live freely and lightly."

The Worrys had never heard such words before.

"Let me see if I have this right, God," said Walt Sr. with wonder in his voice. "We give you our worries and you'll give us the peace that passes perception?"

The Worrys couldn't see God smiling on the other end of the phone, but He was.

"Yes," said God, "That's exactly what I want to give you. Peace— my peace."

"Well, speaking on behalf of all the Worrys, God, I think we'd like to walk and work with You. If you're not too busy right now, could You come over for some waffles?"

And God said, "Oh, I've been waiting for you to ask. I'm on my way. In fact, I'll bring the whipped cream!" ❖

THE Regular Kingdom AND THE Beautiful Kingdom

❦

A fairy tale

for all those who have

peeked over the fence

with longing.

*O*nce, I really believed the world divided up into two kingdoms. One kingdom was regular, and the other kingdom was beautiful.

The Beautiful Kingdom had green rolling hills with a huge river that ran alongside it. There were trees of every kind, crops, livestock, fields full of flowers, and beautifully planned communities with easy-access expressways, all leading to the huge downtown shopping and recreational area.

And, of course, in such a beautiful kingdom there would be beautiful people. They were gorgeous and well-educated, outstanding in manners, character, and citizenship—perfect in every way. Perfectly beautiful!

The mayor was beautiful. The mayor's wife and six children were beautiful. The secretaries, store clerks, butchers, bakers, and barbers, the hair designers, manicurists, facialists, plumbers, painters, preachers, and principals, the teachers, technicians, doctors, dentists, librarians, agrarians and veterinarians, the gardeners, gas station attendants, grandparents, mothers, fathers, children, and even the wrinkled, pink, little newborns— all were beautiful!

The beautiful people of this kingdom knew that people from the other kingdom—The Regular Kingdom—wanted to live in their kingdom.

So, you can imagine how overjoyed I was when I received permission to visit my Aunt Edith in The Beautiful Kingdom.

I am from the other kingdom—The Regular Kingdom. It's nothing like The Beautiful Kingdom. It's kind of normal, average, everyday, unpretentious, ordinary, typical, familiar, commonplace—and terribly regular in The Regular Kingdom.

As the bus drove away from the station that Saturday, the gray, average, regular-shaped buildings, the dull, flat, plain old landscape, the handful of regular well-wishers—my dad, my best friend, and my very regular little brother—got smaller and smaller as I stared out the back window until my kingdom disappeared.

I dozed off and on as we bumped along, and then, after what seemed like hours, I saw it off in the distance. The Beautiful Kingdom! As the bus rolled to a stop, I could hardly take it all in. It was so much more than any description or postcard. I searched the crowd for my aunt. There—there she was! Beautiful. Cool. She hadn't changed at all. She brushed my cheek with a kiss and said those familiar words, "My, how you've grown."

I felt so odd, so ordinary, so regular among all the beauty of this kingdom. My aunt must have sensed this, for she took me on an immediate shopping spree. My own new wardrobe of beautiful clothes with tags and labels that said very important things, not just "100% cotton, wash and tumble dry." I felt less regular each time we bought something.

Then we ate lunch at a real French restaurant. My plate was a picture of beauty, right down to the tomato rose and basil garnish.

Oh, how I enjoyed my first day in this kingdom! The party Aunt Edith gave me was a dream come true. Meeting all the people she knew, swimming in her Olympic-sized pool with a waterfall and spa left me breathless. And my very own room—complete with entertainment center, dressing area, and bathroom—was more than I had ever imagined.

That night, as I slipped between my powder blue silk sheets, something began to change. I knew that night that I never wanted to leave this kingdom.

The next morning I was up early, with my aunt's favorite breakfast set before me. Swallowing my first bite, I ventured, "Aunt Edith, I need to ask you a question."

"My dear, I already know. Who wouldn't want to live in this kingdom? However, the more important question you should be asking is this: 'What must I do to be granted citizenship to The Beautiful Kingdom?'"

The suspense was killing me. I swallowed my last bite of French toast and blurted it out.

"What? Aunt Edith, what do I have to do?"

"Change," she said in a cool, knowing tone.

"Change?"

"Yes, change. Change everything."

"Oh, okay. All right."

"Well, my dear, are you ready to work really hard?"

"Yes!"

"Then let's go!"

She beckoned from the front door with gold and platinum charge cards in hand. And we were off to change, rearrange, mold, manipulate, and remake me. I was willing. I'd made up my mind. I'd do whatever it took to change enough for this kingdom.

The weeks of summer flew by. My aunt found this thing and that thing to change. A complete hair and color analysis had done wonders with my looks. Daily salon visits had changed every hair and nail I owned. An orthodontist was hard at work on a slight overbite. Weekly visits to the dermatologist had cleared up a slight blemish problem. Contacts turned my eyes a lovely shade of blue. A nutritionist had enabled me to whittle away some extra pounds. Modeling classes had improved my posture. And little plastic inserts from the podiatrist had corrected my fallen arches.

My wardrobe had expanded along with my good taste for the finer things. I joined an exclusive health spa. I joined an equestrian group. An art appreciation group. A ballet class. A theater group. And the list went on and on and on. . . .

I could feel it. I could see it. It had happened. I had changed.

The end of the summer came, and it was time for the all-important interview with the mayor.

"A technicality," my aunt assured me. "There's nothing to worry about."

The reception area was quiet that day. Beautiful, but quiet. I sat there alone, nervously thumbing through magazines, checking my reflection, reviewing my first words to the mayor.

I must admit that, as I sat there, I had second thoughts. Had I really changed?

I looked different from the top of my head to the soles of my feet. But had I changed enough? I was interrupted from my doubts by a compliment from the mayor.

"Well, the apple doesn't fall far from the tree. You're just as beautiful as your Aunt Edith."

My confidence was back. I walked like a model from a page out of *Vogue* straight into the mayor's office.

The minute I sat down, the questions started. Question after question about this and that and that and this. I could feel the perspiration on my forehead and oh, how I wished the mayor had offered me a drink of water that day.

Finally, the mayor closed the file he'd been scribbling in and looked right at me.

"Well, my dear, I'm most pleased with the amount of change you've made. There is only one change left involving your signature."

"One more change?" I thought. "What could possibly be left?"

"Just a technicality," said the mayor as he placed the pen in my hand and moved the last page of my file in front of me to sign.

It read:

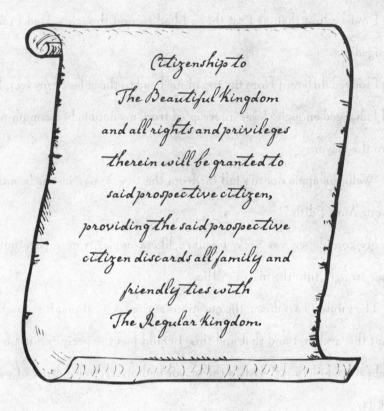

Citizenship to
The Beautiful Kingdom
and all rights and privileges
therein will be granted to
said prospective citizen,
providing the said prospective
citizen discards all family and
friendly ties with
The Regular Kingdom.

. . . providing the said citizen discards all family and friendly ties with The Regular Kingdom. I stared at the paper. I thought, *What is this? Discard my family, my friends? Everyone? What about my aunt? She hasn't discarded me.*

"Is there a problem?" asked the mayor.

I stared at the paper again.

"Well?"

"I . . . I can't. I can't sign your paper!" And I shoved the file back across the desk and started running.

I ran out of that office, out of the beautiful high rise building. I ran past the stores full of beautiful clothes and beautiful things, past all the beautiful people on beautiful streets doing beautiful things—or so it had seemed.

Out of breath, confused, I burst through the door of my aunt's home. She rushed to congratulate me, and I stopped her.

"How come you never come to The Regular Kingdom? I need to know, Aunt Edith. Am I your niece, or am I a relationship you've thrown away in order to live here in The Beautiful Kingdom?"

She just stood there. Beautiful. Cool. Aloof.

"My, how you've grown."

The words came out of her mouth, but they sounded different.

She then brushed my cheek with a kiss and whispered in my ear words I have never forgotten to this day. "You must choose your kingdom, my dear."

I packed my things, said goodbye, and headed for the bus terminal. I was going home, home to where things would be regular again.

The ride back to The Regular Kingdom was as regular as could be. There was *just* a hint of fall in the air. The trees were *just* beginning to display their colors, and everything seemed in harmony with itself on that old regular road—potholes and all.

Then I saw it off in the distance. The faint outline of The Regular Kingdom against the pink of the setting sun. It was like I was seeing it for the very first time. It looked . . . beautiful.

As we neared the bus station, I could see hundreds of citizens. The band from my high school was playing, and a banner was stretched across the crowd. Then I saw my dad, my little brother, and my best friend all waving from the front of the crowd. I looked around the crowd for the mayor, the chief of police, someone important.

Then I saw it! On the banner in huge block letters read my name and the words,

WELCOME HOME, WE LOVE YOU!

There were hugs and kisses and tears. I'd been missed! Regular me!

My dad, little brother, best friend and I all headed home to a Glad-You're-Back-Welcome-Home meal. Oh—no tomato rose and basil garnish on the side of my plate, but the best meal I'd eaten all summer.

It felt good to be home at last. To be with people who see you as you are and accept you—as you are.

I was home, really home . . . in The Regular Kingdom. ♣

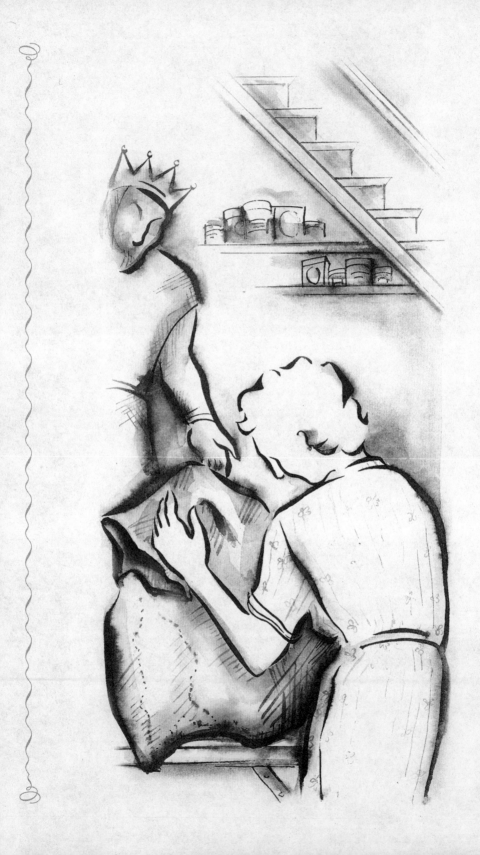

THE
SACK

A story

about

forgiveness

and

letting go.

There once was a woman who lived in a faraway land. Well, actually, she lived right down the street.

She was a good woman, a nice woman, with a husband, two children, a dog, a cat and a small tract home. She was always the courteous sort. Said hi to her neighbors, kept her garden weeded, served on the PTA every year, volunteered at the hospital on Wednesdays, and held the best yard sales, with all the proceeds going to a local charity. Why, she even made Kool-Aid in the summer when no one else's mom would make that stuff.

There was no doubt about it. She was nice. A very nice woman. But there was a secret in her life. A secret guarded and hidden and important. Her secret was a sack. A large, filthy, tattered sack.

Now, she hadn't always had this sack. But over time, she found she needed something. Something for an injustice or two she had suffered. Something for the cross and unkind words tossed her way without thinking. Something for the lie she'd been told by a trusted friend. Something for the relationship that had soured years ago. For the painful childhood memories, regrets, unforgivable mistakes, and her own self-criticism for never measuring up. She needed something for all of that—a container, a sack.

Each night, long after her family had gone off to bed and the sounds of sleep were heard throughout the house—when all was quiet and still— the nice woman would creep down to the cellar of her home. There among the canned peaches and green beans, the rusty bikes, old toys, and dusty boxes, there it was. There, behind some baby furniture, was the sack.

Each night, in her cold, dark, musty sanctuary, she'd heave that heavy sack up on a broken down cardboard table. Then by the dim light of the cellar, she'd revisit the contents almost like dear old friends. She'd pull each one out carefully, reliving the pain, the bitterness, the disappointment, the anger, and the hurt, until she began to whimper and cry, anguish over it all.

Suddenly, a rapping on the cellar door would interrupt her. She knew the knock. It was the King, the Great King. And sometimes, when she heard that knock, she'd scramble upstairs back to bed. Sometimes she'd flick out the light and pretend she wasn't there. Other times, she'd call out to Him, "Door's open. You can come in."

He'd walk right into that place. He'd step over the rusty bikes and old toys, past the shelves of canned peaches and green beans, and the boxes marked "Thanksgiving," "Christmas," and "Easter."

He'd walk right over to the broken down cardboard table where she and the sack were. He'd put His arm around her, draw her close, stroke her hair, wipe away all the tears, and ask for the sack.

She'd nod a yes to Him. And He'd sweep away all of it—the bitterness, the disappointment, the anger, and hurt—off the table, into the sack and shoulder it away with Him.

A feeling of lightness always followed the Great King's leaving with the sack. It was wonderful! It lasted for days and weeks, sometimes months. No more stealing down to the cellar, no more crying, no more sack.

Then she'd remember. A small something would trigger a memory about the soured relationship, the painful childhood experience, a self-doubt. And the bitterness, disappointment, anger, and hurt would rush in on her. She'd need the sack. She'd want the sack. She'd go and get the sack back from the Great King.

Again, He would knock gently, come in, wipe away the tears, and take back the sack. And again, she would go and get it back from Him.

This went on for many years until one day she stopped leaving the cellar door unlatched for the Great King. Leaves and debris piled up around the unused door. Eventually, she learned to close her ears to the gentle rapping that continued night after night after night.

And time went by. The nice woman grew old, tired, small, and frail. Her husband died, leaving her well cared for. Her two children grew up, married, and moved away. Then someone else weeded the garden, held the yard sales, and made all the Kool-Aid in the summer. And the sack? Oh, it was still a part of her life. Larger, filthier, more tattered and heavy, so very heavy for her.

One day last summer her daughter called to talk. The phone rang and rang and rang. Her daughter got worried, called her brother, and asked him to go check on their mother.

He did. He checked everywhere. He called the authorities. They checked everywhere but never found the nice woman—just a big, old, filthy, tattered sack, propped up in an easy chair.

There once was a woman who lived in a faraway land. Well, actually, she lived right down the street. ❖

Letting the Story
Speak to Us

A story is a very friendly visitor.

It knocks gently on the front door of our hearts.

We readily let it in with an, "Oh, it's you. Come on in!"

And pretty soon it is telling us things about life

And the way we live that we hadn't quite expected from such a simple guest.

Wonderful things happen when we can suspend our inner critic and know we are safe to tell what a story has meant to us. Over the years, I have used my stories in discussions with small groups, retreats, classes, Bible studies, workshops, and staff gatherings. The results are always the same. The time spent is always rich in the understanding of the story and rich in a kind of relating that builds people.

My hope is that you will want to take some of my stories into your group settings and spend time discussing them. As you use stories in this way, remember this: a kind, gentle, and open discussion can be very freeing and reinforcing of our own story and those sharing in a discussion with us. A listener's positive, non-verbal cues assure us of the value of both ourselves and our story. It's a great opportunity and gift to be heard and to listen.

Here are some ways to create a comfortable climate for looking more deeply into a story:

- If your group is large enough to break up into groups, keep the number limited to five.

- It's a simple thing, but facing one another at a table or forming a circle creates openness. Take care in spacing groups away from one another to maximize listening and a sense of personal space for each group.

- Allow time for discussion. And as you discuss, give people time to think through a question. Silence between responses is not a bad thing. People are processing.

- As you begin, I want to caution you to suspend comments about people's thoughts and answers concerning a story. Respect and guard the discussion. What was shared was intended for your gathering, your group. Remind people that there are no right or wrong answers when we reflect on a story. Keep in mind that there is something sacred about your time spent in a small group discussion. You are giving and receiving one another's stories, and that is always a priceless thing.

🎗 Try plying some creative art activity with your story discussion. It could involve a collage made from magazine pictures, colored pencils, crayons and paper, or modeling clay. The right and left brain engage when we create with our hands. You'll find that the discussion will be lively and in-depth with this visual context added.

I enjoy discussing stories with children. When you do this, keep in mind that their answers will be more immediate and simple than adults'. Understand, though, that this does not mean their answers lack the depth of an adult's. To the contrary, these little ones are much more comfortable with using imagination and less jaded by life's experiences. Children possess less history and perspective. By 10 or 11, children are able to think in dualities and uncover the meaning behind an object, a person, or a situation. When you use these questions with children in a group setting, lay down the same kind of *rules* for discussion as you would for adults. Also, use these questions in family or evening story times with your children. There is something about the end of the day that is disarming for children and adults alike.

The following questions can be used with adults and children. I have used them for years. The questions start at an easy and open place and can move forward to a deeper level of sharing. Use them in any way you prefer. This is only a jumping-off place.

One more absolutely important thing: have fun!

Adult-Friendly Questions

- What is your immediate response—*your gut reaction*—to this story?
- Was there a character in the story that you related to the most? Why?
- What does this story tell you about yourself?
- What does this story tell you about God?
- How will this story make a difference in the way you approach your life, your family, your spouse, your friends, or people in general?

Child-Friendly Questions

- What did this story make you feel?
- What character did you like the most? Why?
- What was your favorite part of the story?
- What did God say to you in this story?
- What do you think happened next in the story?
- Does this story remind you of another story? Tell us about it.

THE GIANTS WITHOUT Manners

❦

In the Land of

Fee-Fi-Fo-Fum &

Fiddle-Dee-Dee,

There lived some Giants

who never said,

"I'm sorry, thank you, or please."

In the Land of Fee-Fi-Fo-Fum and Fiddle-Dee-Dee,

There lived some giants who never said, "I'm sorry, thank you, or please."

They were rude and crude and an awful sloppy bunch,

And they made noises and messes when they ate their lunch.

When they were out walking they left trails full of trash,

And people knew to stay clear or their feets would get smashed.

"We will not say it, no way," the giants would grumble.

"It's dumb! Just try to make us, and you'll take a tumble!"

So they went through life rudely, just thumbing their noses,

Never saying "thank you," "I'm sorry," or "please" to one single soulses.

Their families all cried. Their friends all complained,

"We taught them. What happened? I guess we're to blame."

So that's how it was for the longest of time,

And these giants ruled the land and thought life was just fine.

And then one day to the surprise of all in this land

There appeared a fairy with a special book in her hand.

"Ah-hem!" she said as she cleared her throat,

"I've been sent by the Big Guy who gave me this note.

"'Go to the Land of Fiddle-Dee-Dee and Fee-Fi-Fo-Fum

And take care of the giants who are acting like bums!'

"So come out, come out wherever you are

There's no need to hide from a fairy with a star!"

Then all of a sudden from behind some big rocks

Came the giants without manners in their smelly, dirty socks.

"Yeah, what do you want? We're trying to sleep!

Is this some joke?" And they rolled up their sleeves.

"No, no, no, it's no joke," she smiled a smile most merry.

"I've been sent by the Big Guy. I'm the Good Manners Fairy."

"We don't care who you are or who sent you to this place.

Take that book and that wand and get out of our face.

"'Cause we're the Giants *Without* Manners, and we do what we please.

Besides you're no bigger than a little, tiny flea!"

"Pardon me," said the fairy with a smile *not* so merry.

"But what you just said was mean and cruel and very,

"Impolite, unfriendly, childish, and crude,

Not to mention disdainful, wartish, and rude.

"And now, I'd like an apology, a handshake, and a how do you do.

We're going to be friends, my dear giants. It's long overdue."

The giants just stood there with a look of shock on their faces.

That little tiny fairy had put them all in their places.

She was right. They *were* mean, unfriendly, and crude,

Impolite, disdainful, wartish, and rude.

They felt all these feelings that now rumbled and tumbled,

And their thoughts were new thoughts that seemed to unjumble.

"An apology, a hand shake and a how do you do?'

No one's ever been this nice." And the giants cried, "Boo-hoo!"

Then up from the bottom of their hearts came a word.

A word that they'd heard and once thought absurd.

The Giants Without Manners could now understand.

So they all took a big breath and stuck out one hand.

"Sorry!"

It was loud. It was big. It was long. It was clear.

They meant it, they said it! In fact it was dear.

And the fairy with a smile and eyes very watery,

Said, "That's it big guys. You've ended your thuggery.

"Just one more change, though, is needed on this special day,

A name that describes you without cliché."

She opened the special book she had brought with her wand

And pondered some big thoughts for these oversized ones.

She thought and she thought and it took more than an hour,

To come up with a name that would be more than a wow-er.

By now the Land of Fee-Fi-Fo-Fum and Fiddle-Dee-Dee

Had all gathered in the main square to hear this decree.

The fairy shut the Big Book and closed her eyes real tight,

She seemed to be talking to Someone with all of her might.

"Uh-huh, I got that. Oh, yes, You are right.

They're sorry, in fact, they said it with all their might."

Then opening her eyes wide she said, "Oh it's beautiful!

"You'll love it. It's perfect. It describes every part of you!"

The giants were all bending on their giant sized knees,

Waiting, anticipating their new name with great glees.

"Your name shall be remembered from now until always

As *The Giants of Mercy, Kindness, and First-Aid.*"

The giants were silent. All the people were too.

It was a name filled with promise and tons of virtue.

"We accept it. We thank you. We'll wear it with pride."

And they stood up to applause that could be heard far and wide.

For the Giants Without Manners had changed on that day,

To The Giants of Mercy, Kindness, and First Aid!

So next time you see these giants don't be surprised whatsoever,

If you find them loving, delightful, helpful, and absolutely clever. ✤

THE LAND

OF

Sighs

A sigh can be a

very telling thing.

Its volume deafening

or delicious.

Its meaning

disapproving or dear.

*T*here once was a land where people sighed all the time, about everything. A sigh meant many, many things in this land: "I'm bored, fatigued, upset, put out, put off, dissatisfied, disapproving, disoriented, disorganized, disturbed, or disgusted." There are other sighs that mean "oh, how lovely," but those sighs were rarely heard. Most of the time, sadly, here (I mean there) it meant something altogether (sigh) different.

As you know, to sigh is to exhale, breathe out, expire. It's a pulling in of oxygen and a release of carbon dioxide that completes the sigh. It's not a loud sound. Nor is a sigh quiet. But it's certainly noticeable. And meant to be noticed. In fact, I would venture to say that a sigh is much more vocal in public than in private. And can be dragged out in great length and vocal variation depending on the amount of oxygen one has inhaled. For example: [Give a short sigh and long sigh.]

Now, in this Land of Sighs there lived a Sigh-er of Sighers—The Queen of the Sighs—a woman who'd been sighing all of her life. She was well into her eighties. They called her affectionately Granny Mona (and boy could she moan!). She'd begun sighing as a small child, as a little bitty thing. It was over someone who took something out of her hand for some reason. She couldn't, for the life of her, remember what it was, but she started sighing way back then.

She'd sigh about everything: the weather, what she ate for breakfast, the cost of pickles, prescriptions and Polygrip, her aches and pains, postal workers, the president, the news, the schools, her family, her friends, the neighbors, her city, her church, her pastor, and the people who filled the pews.

Then one bright sunny Sunday in August (hot enough to sigh about), her pastor opened the Good Book to the gospel of Mark and told the story of the deaf and mute man. This man had never heard a sigh in all of his life. He'd never uttered a sigh in all his life. He had a speech problem (a deaf man with a speech impediment, it says in the Good Book). Well, people brought the man to Jesus and begged Him to heal their friend. So Jesus led the man to a private place, a quiet place, away from all those people.

He then placed his fingers in the man's ears. Then Jesus spit onto His own fingers and touched the man's tongue with (that's right) His own spit. And looking up into Heaven, Jesus *sighed* and commanded, "Be opened now!" Instantly, the man could hear perfectly and speak plainly!

Granny Mona thought about that miraculous story all day. It bothered her, and she sighed through lunch and all the way to dinner. Her sighs had never healed one person. Her sighs had never amounted to one prayer. They were complaints and definitions and critiques and defenses. They were the words that spoke volumes, thousands of words that she never really had to be responsible for saying. So on that bright sunny Sunday in August, in a private place, the quiet place of her own home with only Jesus present, she asked Him to lay His hands on her mouth, and she stopped sighing. Not one more sigh was heard from her 89-year-old mouth. And God let her live 10 more years, not because she had quit sighing, but because she had so much to say about Him.

And did the Land of Sighs change? They talk more now. And the sighs are mostly for different reasons now. There are sighs of . . .

"Oh, how lovely."

"Oh, thank you."

"Oh, how beautiful."

"Oh, what a surprise."

"Oh, I love you."

"Oh, I miss you."

"Oh, I long for you."

"Oh, I'm sooo content."

And those sighs mean something altogether different, don't they? ♣

THE Fountain

An allegory about a

Great Fountain

and living water never

tasted before.

Once upon a time there was a land and a people that had been valued beyond compare. They had been given a Great Fountain. Right in the center of their land was a beautiful fountain out of which living water flowed. Oh, yes. It really was living water! One drink could change a person altogether.

Now, I don't think it changed a big nose to a small nose or erased a few unwanted pounds, but it did change people. It took away the thirsts of life. Ears that had never really heard, heard. Eyes that had never really seen, saw. And hearts that had been hardened through and through could be changed altogether by one taste of that living water.

Every day, every person came for water. Some in the morning, some at noon, and some in the cool of the evening. That drink seemed to make all the difference in their lives. And it was enough.

Over time though, some stopped coming for water. As unbelievable as this may sound, some began skipping days here and there. Some decided they needed the water only once or twice a year, not every day. Some came only when their friends did. In fact, it became so unpopular that those few who still went for water snuck out for a quick drink after dark, when no one was watching.

And then it happened. No one came to the Great Fountain for water.

Time wore on in this land, until the Fountain became a part of history. A vague memory. The path to it became overgrown with weeds and brush. The water turned dark and still. Finally, it dried up.

And so did the people. They gradually preferred the company of dark rooms, the safety of locked doors, and the comfort of barred windows. A mute-like existence took over their lives. They were alone, afraid, and oh so very thirsty.

One of the very last things they did to erase the Fountain from their memories was to hide it. They wanted it gone. It was quite a task, this hiding. A huge wall replaced the rolling landscape as new boundaries to the land were established. Plans were drawn, mortar poured, bricks laid, until at last, the Fountain was no longer inside their land.

One day, one hot, dusty day in August, a healer sent by the Great King reached this land. He had been traveling a long time to get to this place. He was hungry and tired when He passed through tethered gates. Strangely, to this man, their gates, locked doors, and barred windows were gestures of welcome—an invitation to restore, cleanse, heal.

There was no outward notice taken of His presence that day, but they were watching Him—from around corners, behind cracked doors, through scraps of curtains—hoping He'd pass through one gate and out the other and leave their land.

The Healer came to what appeared to be a forgotten inn or a motel. Its rusty sign swung back and forth in the breeze. He had been standing at the front desk ringing the bell for a while when a man poked his head through a curtained doorway a few feet away. Squinting from the change in light from one room to the next, he grumbled, "Forty dollars in advance."

The man was young but looked worn, so worn, as if life had passed him by in some sort of unfair way. He was careful to avoid the Healer's eyes as he took the money and gave directions. "Room's at the top. Check-out's at noon."

"I won't be leaving tomorrow," said the Healer. "I'll be staying a while."

But the man knew better. The last visitor had left before nightfall. Yet this stranger seemed different. His voice and His appearance were somehow familiar, although the man was sure he'd never met Him before.

Maybe He would stay, thought the man, maybe. Catching himself mid-thought, he retreated to the safety and company of his TV.

The Healer put His things away and then was off to find food and some answers. It was dusk now and through the filminess of the ending day, He saw people walking just ahead of Him. He called out to them. No answer. They were there, somewhere in the shadows, watching Him.

Then He saw it. A square little building with a marquee blinking "Diner." The lights were on, the door was open but, like the motel, it was deserted.

"Hello. Hello, is anyone here?"

No answer. He was about to leave when a little old lady came out of the kitchen, waving a dirty dish towel. "Just a minute. Just a minute."

An uncontrollable cough took over her frail body. The Healer hurried to her side, steadied her with His strong arms. "Please, let me help you."

"I don't need any help. We have enough help around here." She knew the stranger had meant something else. "Sit down. I'll send out some food."

And once inside the safety of the dark kitchen, she got a good look at Him. She was still holding her arm where the Healer had touched her. His touch had gone right through her, to a place long ago in her life. It felt warm, somehow familiar.

"Get him some food!"

With that command, a young girl, wild in appearance, danced her way to the Healer's table. She stopped only long enough to place a cup and a bowl in front of Him.

"What's your name?" asked the Healer.

No answer. She was totally absorbed in a crazy kind of twirling and spinning and twirling and spinning.

"You dance beautifully." Again, no response.

His eyes were fixed upon her now. "Who taught you?"

At that question, she stopped. Her eyes met the Healer's eyes. She seemed calm now as she took a few cautious stops toward Him. She stamped her feet and quickly signed something with her hands.

"Please," said the Healer. "I want to understand you."

Locked in His gaze, she stamped her feet and signed something again and again and again. Suddenly, an angry howl filled the diner. "Get in here, you lazy girl! Get these dishes done!"

The wild look returned and she twirled her way back into the darkness.

The Healer ate in silence, paid His check to an empty counter, and spoke into the darkness of the kitchen. "I'll be back. Tomorrow. Goodbye."

The old woman felt her arm again. She wished the stranger had stayed longer. Did He know her time was short? How could He? He was only a stranger, with no business asking about her health.

The girl wiped the steam off the window above the sink. She could barely make out His silhouette against the night sky, but a part of Him had been etched into her memory. His soft, warm eyes were somehow familiar. In the moment, she'd felt peace she'd never known before. The thought of His return made her happy. She would find a way to talk to Him tomorrow.

The Healer walked back to the inn with weariness tugging at every step. The Great King's words made sense now. He had told Him they would be stubborn. He had told Him they would be fearful. He had told Him they would be angry and sad. The Great King had also told Him, "It will be their choice."

He wished "Good night" to the man peeking though the curtain and waited on the steps for a like response. Nothing. "Tomorrow," He whispered over and over as He plodded up the stairs. "Tomorrow, I'll find it."

The morning light betrayed what the night had hidden so well. The land and buildings, which seemed empty and forgotten, weren't. Everyone knew there was a stranger now. A stranger in their land who would not leave. As He passed by their dwellings, doors clicked to lock and windows were shut and latched tight.

He was determined. He was going to find what was lost. And once He found it—well, just as the Great King had told Him, "It will be their choice."

He was thinking about that when His feet fell upon a worn path that ended just inside the walls of the land. Peering through some cracks, He saw more of the path on the other side. Something inside of Him knew this was it. He scaled the huge stone wall, leapt to the ground on the other side, and started clearing the path, trampling whatever weeds He could, pulling out all the rest. Finally, He reached it. It was the fountain.

"It must have been beautiful." His fingers traced the once intricately carved edge, now caked with dust and decay. "Beautiful."

The Healer knew exactly where He was now. He stared into the dryness of the Fountain, overwhelmed with what had been lost, neglected, unwanted. Tears rolled down the Healer's face, wetting the dusty edge of the Fountain. The tears then turned into weeping, a weeping that overcame the Healer until He collapsed over the edge of the Fountain. The sobs that shook His body turned into a wailing lament. It was as if the Healer had been wounded to the very deepest part of His being.

It was an awful sound, a wounded sound. No one in the land could ignore it. It moved through the weeds and brush. Found its way past the mortar and bricks. It crept under the locked doors and through the barred windows. It went straight though the thick walls of their homes until, at last, it penetrated the very hands that covered their ears to shut it out.

It was so strange. The cry seemed to be calling them, by name.

One by one, the cry drew them. The worn man from the motel, the little old woman from the diner, and the crazy, twirling girl. One by one, the people came.

The cry drew them outside their land. Drew them to a cleared path that had not been walked in many years. To a path that led them to a dry and empty Fountain—and a Healer.

The years of trying to forget, of trying desperately to shove it to the very farthest part of their memories, were over. Now they knew why the Healer had come. And one by one, each made a choice.

Some fell to the ground and buried their faces. Some bowed their knees and closed their eyes. Some stared into the emptiness of the Fountain. Oh, how they wanted it back. They wanted to drink from the Fountain once again.

Lost in their thoughts and tears, they hadn't noticed that the crying had subsided from the Healer and that He was now straightening up, ready to speak.

"This time," He spoke in clear, inviting syllables. "This time, taste the water." And He touched the edge of the Fountain and was gone.

Now they felt a low rumbling beneath their feet. Then water shot from the spout, soaking everyone to the bone. The water ran down into a beautiful marble fountain etched with fine silver and gold.

In only moments, the pool below the fount was filled to the top. The people stared with wonder at what had been given back. Then, helping one another to their feet, they began to give drinks of water to each other with cupped hands.

This time, they tasted the water. It was cool, soothing, almost sweet. They had never tasted anything like it before. They let it run down their chins, then washed their faces, hands, and feet. And they drank and drank and tasted and tasted and drank and tasted.

That day, they broke down the wall that stood in the way of their Fountain. And that day, ears that had never really heard, heard. Eyes that had never really seen, saw. And hearts hardened through and through were changed. Forever.

All by one taste of living water from a Great Fountain. ✤

THE Land

OF

Stinky Feet

This story was written

while I worked with high school people.

I wanted them to know how very

special they are in God's kingdom.

I wanted to encourage their servants' hearts.

May it do the same for you.

There once was a land called The Land of Stinky Feet, and it truly was once . . . stinky! No one seemed to know it, though, for the longest time. In fact, they denied it, lied about it, pretended, and ignored it. Until one young man named Ernest confronted all that. But wait, I'm getting ahead of the story.

The Land of Stinky Feet didn't start out stinky. They say the land smelled of roses and lilacs. When the breeze was just right, people across the valley could smell the wonderful floral fragrances wafting their way from the land. Well, that's because, of course, no one's feet smelled back then. Back then, they were footwashers. Yes, footwashers!

You see, a long time ago, a Footwasher dropped by their land with shiny wash bins, fresh Turkish towels, cakes of soaps, lotions, and powders.

He set up camp down by the river. And to their surprise, he didn't seem to be selling anything. He just wanted to wash a foot or two.

His touch was gentle, the soap was creamy, the lotions were soothing. Ingrown toenails, calluses, and corns—gone! Hammertoes, heel spurs, bunions—healed! Dry, flaky, itchy feet—treated! The gunk between the toes—disappeared! Sore, aching, tired muscles—massaged!

The people of this land had been taking care of their feet for years: scrubbing, scraping, medicating. But after the Footwasher, well, nobody had ever experienced these kind of feet. It was amazing! It was wonderful! Their washed feet seemed to change their whole person. In fact, getting your feet washed by the Footwasher was the best part of the whole day.

Orderly lines of young and old alike would begin to form down by the river around seven in the morning, with the last big toe dried about midnight. They spent hours with the Footwasher. They fed him well, gave him a little cottage to stay in, and generously paid him for his services.

Then came the dreadful day that no one had anticipated: the Footwasher announced that he had to move on.

"Why? Who will wash our feet like you do?" the people asked.

"I can show you how," he said with a smile and a twinkle in his eyes. "And if each person washes one pair a feet a day, your feet will forever feel wonderful. Come, follow me down to the river and see."

Everyone took part that day and they were quite excited to find out that it wasn't as hard as they had imagined. Willingness, tender care, and the right footwashing equipment were all that was really necessary. In fact, washing feet was as good as getting one's feet washed. There was such a feeling of helpfulness and accomplishment, and the thank-you's fell on the ears so nicely.

Sadly, the day came when, early in the morning, the Footwasher had to leave. Everyone helped him pack up his things and followed him to the edge of town to wave a bittersweet goodbye.

"Remember, ten toes, two arches, two soles a day," he yelled to the crowd with a twinkle in his eyes.

"We will! Ten toes, two arches, two soles a day! Ten toes, two arches, two soles a day . . . ," and soon he disappeared over the hills.

Everyone stood there feeling a bit empty and sad 'til the crackly voice of an adolescent spoke up. "Well, let's get started!" It was Ernest, a boy not more than 12 or 13. But just the same, all the people grabbed their basins, towels, soap, lotion, and foot powder and off they went into their day.

Now the Footwasher had said, "You'll know which pair to wash if you look with your heart instead of with your eyes." So that's what they did, and the first day went very well indeed. Everyone's feet got washed! It was amazing! Not one single toe had been left untouched, from the tiniest newborn to Old Grandpa Duncan.

The next day, same thing. Everyone's feet got washed. It was as if the people had been washing feet all their lives. It was a little bit embarrassing when someone asked to wash your feet, especially if you were new to the land. But your feet felt so splendid afterwards, and the footwasher felt so splendid, that it was worth the cost of a few pink cheeks.

Some of the best footwashers in the land were the children. They weren't afraid to ask, "Have you had your feet washed today?" And they giggled and chattered and the soap bubbles went everywhere as people received the specialness of a child's touch.

And the older the footwasher, the more gentle and careful they were with a person's feet. They listened as they washed. They made the owner of the feet feel very important. I think it was the wisdom of age. "After all, you want a pair that'll last a lifetime, don't you?" they'd say.

And life went on and on, day to day—ten toes, two arches, two soles a day.

But, as I said earlier, things changed in this land. You're not going to believe this, but some people lied about having had their feet washed. Footwashers slacked off and said, "I'll wash an extra pair tomorrow." Some decided to hide behind spanking new shoes and fancy socks and stockings. Some preferred certain footwashers to other footwashers.

Some made up excuses. "Why don't you go wash my neighbor's feet first?" or "My feet are still clean from yesterday." And some just flat-out refused to wash or be washed!

Well, little by little, an aroma began to fill the land of the footwashers. A smell that was old and stale, like a gym locker that hadn't been cleaned out all year. Like a pair of sneakers that had been worn and worn, but never washed. Worse than Limburger cheese and rotten eggs. The smell grew pungent and acrid, burning to the nostrils, but no one noticed it. Not one person!

As the smell grew, the sound of "Ten toes, two arches, two soles a day" faded. The little town downwind could hardly take it on a breezy day. They started calling that land "The Land of Stinky Feet!" In fact, they kept clothespins in their pockets for just such breezy days.

Ernest was one of the few willing footwashers left in the land. He'd load up his basin, towel, and soap along with his books and lunch. He was a senior in high school now and he'd become rather sad and disheartened about footwashing. The daily refusals were almost more than he could bear. Even his parents disagreed with him. "Is footwashing worth all this?" But sometimes he'd get a vision of the Gentle Footwasher. "Ten toes, two arches, two soles a day!" And he'd try again.

Another fall was approaching in The Land of Stinky Feet. Ernest had been accepted to a university on the other side of the valley, and one Indian summer day, he loaded up some duffel bags in his VW and kissed his mom and dad goodbye. "See you at the break."

"Going to miss you, son," said his mother.

"Me, too," said his dad, "but not all the talk and pressure about footwashing."

Ernest drove all day, and by early evening he reached the sleepy college town and stopped at a diner. He sat down at the counter next to a man reading a newspaper.

Soon a waitress appeared with a menu and an aerosol can. "Here you go. Special's meatloaf, and do you smell that?"

"Smell what?"

"I don't know, kind of like old gym socks, really old gym socks?" She spritzed the air a few times. "Do you smell it, Doc?" She was talking to the man at the counter next to Ernest as she spritzed the air again. The Doc just looked at Ernest.

"Well, that should take care of it. What'll you have, son? Our cheeseburgers are the best in town!"

"Make it a double cheeseburger, French fries, chocolate malt, and a slab of that apple pie a la mode, please."

Ernest sat there drinking his ice water. "Boy, I sure don't smell anything." The gentleman folded his paper and smiled at Ernest as the waitress placed their orders in front of them. "Enjoy, Doc—and you, too, kid."

"Excuse me," said Ernest, reaching across the counter for napkins. "Are you a real doctor?"

"Yes."

"What kind of doctor?"

"I teach at the university here in town."

"Really? I'm a first semester freshman!"

"Well, you won't find a better school for podiatry."

"Podiatry? What's that?"

"The specialized care of feet. In fact, I could take care of that problem of yours in about a half-hour's treatment."

"What problem?"

"Son, your feet stink."

"What?!"

"Your feet smell."

"My feet smell?!"

"Your feet smell. That's what the waitress was complaining about."

"I don't smell it. I really don't smell it!"

"That's the problem with stinky feet. People don't always know they have 'em. When was the last time you changed shoes?"

"These are new shoes!"

"Hmmm. When was the last time someone washed your feet?"

Ernest was silent.

"My office is nearby, son."

On the walk over, Ernest explained the story of the Footwasher and what had happened to their land over the last several years. He couldn't recall the last time someone had washed his feet.

The doctor listened patiently as Ernest poured out his heart. At his office, he soaked, bathed, lotioned, and powdered the boy's feet. The touch was gentle and familiar to Ernest. He looked down at the man crouched before him with the towels over his arms, his silver basin flashing. Then it hit Ernest.

The face was older and bearded, and there was a small bald spot on top of his head, but six years changes a person's looks. His heart started to pound. Could it be? The gentle doctor then looked up into the hopeful teenager's face. And Ernest's heart leapt.

The Doctor's eyes smiled and out came those familiar words of long ago, "Remember? Ten toes, two arches, two soles a day?"

Ernest remembered. Spontaneous tears poured from his eyes as he stumbled to his feet to hug the Footwasher.

"I knew it was you! All of a sudden, I just knew it was you."

"It's me. It's me, son. Sit down, Ernest." He handed him a fresh pair of cotton socks, sat on a small stool across from Ernest and looked right into his eyes.

"You know, Ernest, I teach a course here called Intro to Podiatry. I think you'll find some answers to what happened in your land. And I know you'll learn more about your own feet."

"I'll take it!"

"Nothing would please me more. Now remember, ten toes, two arches, two soles a day."

"I will. Ten toes, two arches, two soles a day."

The phrase hummed in Ernest's head as he walked back to the diner to pick up his car. When he got there, Ernest discovered an old man sitting at the bus stop near his VW. The old man was looking right into Ernest's car and scratching his head.

"Hi," blurted Ernest. "How are you?"

"Pretty good. Your car?"

"Yes, sir."

"Noticed your towels and basin in there—sure could use a foot-washing."

"What did you say?"

"I said I need my feet washed, son."

It had been a long time since Ernest had washed someone's feet. His hands shook and he got soap in his eyes, but the feeling was exhilarating. It felt wonderful to wash feet.

"I'm sorry, but I'm a little out of practice."

"You did great, son. Thanks—thanks for taking the time to wash an old man's toes."

The semester seemed to fly by. The gentle Footwasher, or "Doc" as the students called him, asked Ernest to dinner the last night of final exams week. The diner was packed, but the two of them found a booth in the very back. And over double cheeseburgers, fries, chocolate malts, and apple pie a la mode, the Footwasher said, "Ernest, it's time to go back home and tell them what you've learned."

The thought made Earnest's stomach do a flip flop. "I know. But I don't think anyone's going to listen to a 19-year-old. I feel all alone. I'm scared."

"I know you are, but it's time to tell them about their feet. Who will tell them if you don't?"

And in that moment Ernest caught a glimpse of the future of those he loved. Eternal stinky feet!

"Ernest," the Footwasher whispered, "They already know about their stinky feet. Somewhere inside they know. You're ready."

The next morning, Ernest loaded up his VW and took off for The Land of Stinky Feet. Miles before he was close to the land, he smelled it. Sour, acrid, and burning to the nostrils. But Ernest was determined. He parked his car and went straight into the house.

He hugged his mom and dad and asked if they'd take a walk with him down to the river. They were thrilled to have their son home again. Of course they'd take a walk.

He sat there on the rocks for a long time with the two of them. He poured out his heart and told them all he had learned about his own stinky feet. And to the surprise of one 19-year-old, two parents, 48 and 50 years old, peeled off their socks and shoes and stuck their feet out in front of a young footwasher, saying, "Scrub away, son, scrub away."

Ernest's hands were shaking, just as on the day he washed the old man's feet outside the diner. He pulled out the soaps, lotions, and powders and untied a towel from around his waist. His parents talked about their years of neglect and pride and stubbornness as their son gently soaked, bathed, lotioned, and powdered their feet.

"Please forgive us," came the words in a whisper with a sniffle. "Oh son, please forgive us."

The moon was full that night and a crispy, cold wind had begun to blow at that very moment of confession, sending the smell of The Land of Stinky Feet right back into their noses. It was awful! Worse than ever before. It kind of got stuck in your nose and throat when you breathed, and it burned.

"Hard to believe we couldn't smell that before."

"That's the problem with stinky feet, Mom. People don't always know they have 'em!"

Ernest helped his parents to their feet. They hugged for a long time, a hug that said a thousand words.

"Well, what's next, son?" They were done, and yet they were beginning again.

"Well, Dad, we each go find a pair of feet to wash."

And turning around, they began to climb up the rocks to the bank of the river. But their confessions of stinky feet had been carried along with that pungent wind. And those who had ears to hear and a nose to smell remembered the gentle Footwasher and the river.

Once Ernest and his parents reached the clearing above the river bed, they heard familiar voices and approaching feet.

"Grandpa Duncan, is that you?"

"Yes indeedy, it's me. Whew! Probably smelled me coming. Oh, Ernest, I need my feet washed. Grandma Duncan couldn't make it all the way to the river. She's back there sitting, but I promised her I'd be back to wash her feet lickety-split."

"How about ours?" said other familiar voices in that small crowd. It was Mr. and Mrs. Gray, dear friends of the family. Ernest's parents stepped into view.

"We'd be glad to wash your feet."

It was amazing! It was a miracle! They were coming in little groups of twos and threes. They carried dusty pans, dingy towels, soaps, lotions, and powders long forgotten, but they were coming.

The winds of change were blowing in The Land of Stinky Feet. And they say the winds of change are blowing still. ♣

The Benefits of a Good Story

"I haven't relaxed like that in a long time," remarked a grown man

carrying a slumbering child after one of my Storynight concerts.

"I guess I needed this even more than she did."

I love telling stories to children. They are eager and ready for a story told over and over again. I love telling stories to teenagers and young adults. They have intensity and honesty in their listening, once they let down their guard. And I love telling stories to adults. They unfold their arms, shut off the voices of responsibility, and simply drink in the luxury of listening and being still.

Remember that prescription of one restoring story a day? Over the years, I've been compiling a list of the benefits of storytelling. Here's what story can do for you:

- It lifts the spirit.

- It brings on a sense of relaxation.

- It's intimate. It's face-to-face.

- It provides a moment to use one's imagination.

- It makes us better active listeners.

- It allows an adult to become like a child. This is a good thing.

- It encourages reading.

- It encourages creative writing.

- It stops the royal rat race if only for the moments of that story.

- It helps us all realize that we are more alike than we are different.

- It maintains the history in a relationship, a family, a group, a nation.

- It tells us, in indirect ways, that we matter to this world.

- It builds hope in us.

- It creates community.

- It gathers a diverse group of people into one place for one purpose.

- It turns off the electronic high-tech of our culture and restores human connection.

- It is one of the best teaching methods around.

- It opens the door for God to speak to us.

- It becomes a mirror into oneself.

- It lends us a perspective on our lives.

I love my work. The privilege of standing before a group of people and telling stories will never become mundane and boring for me. In fact, the longer I tell stories the more I understand their restoring nature. Our driven and busy culture needs and longs for the restoration a story can bring to it. In the short moments of its telling, a story can bring a release to those greater things we are meant to live out, the greater things we are called to be in this life.

THE GRUDGE

BEARER

Pick up a good-sized stone

and hold it in your hand

to feel its weight

as you read this story.

A Grudge is a heavy thing to carry. Ever carried one? On average, a fully developed grudge weighs two to three pounds—close to the weight of a small sack of sugar or flour. Not really heavy, but try carrying it every day, taking it everywhere you go, keeping it close at hand. After a while, it gets exhausting to the bearer of the grudge.

I once knew a man who bore a grudge. He'd carried it most of his life. He'd received it as a child. Not the kind of thing any kid would ever want. It didn't start out as a grudge though. It was a deep wound. A deep wounding from something he had suffered at the hands of someone he loved and trusted.

At first, he carried the wound around for a few days. And the person who had wounded him so very much never even saw his hurt and pain.

Never ever asked forgiveness. And that deepened the wound. And so he carried it into the next week. And the week after that. And the week after that. And with time this wound slowly turned into a grudge—a grudge that he bore with a smirk and a warning to his soul: "No one will ever do that to me again, because I will never forget what happened to me."

The little boy grew into a teenager, and he carried his grudge in his pocket. He grew into a young man, and he carried his grudge with him in his backpack. He grew into a man and he carried his grudge with him in his briefcase—next to his digital organizer, pager, and cell phone.

By now he'd grown more insulated from insults and injuries. No one hurt him because no one ever got close enough.

Then one fresh spring day while on an early morning jog, with his grudge in hand (and his side aching from the extra weight), he met a Stranger as he jogged along. A Stranger with penetrating, friendly eyes, the kind that look like they're smiling all the time.

The Stranger asked, "Can I run with you a bit?"

Not accustomed to this kind of a gesture he said guardedly, "Okay."

They jogged in quiet for blocks . . . miles—the man with the grudge and the Stranger with the smiling eyes.

And then in breathless words the Stranger asked, "Can I carry that rock for you?"

"What rock?" the man with the grudge asked in bewilderment.

"The one you're holding in your hand," said the Stranger.

The man stopped running and opened the sweaty hand that was tightly clenched around his grudge. There it was. A stone—cold, hard, smooth from wear in places. Jagged and rough in others. Dark and nondescript in color. The man couldn't speak. He stared at what he held as if beholding it for the first time.

"I don't understand."

"I do," said the Stranger. "You've carried it a long time, haven't you?"

As if remembering now, he said, "Yes, all my life." He said it while choking back the emotion welling up inside of him.

"You don't have to carry it anymore if you give it to me." And the Stranger held out a hand to him.

Anger rose, mingled with the pain of remembrance, and he shouted, "What good is it to you? It didn't happen to you."

"Yes, it did." And the Stranger opened His hand wider and revealed a scar shaped just like the man's pain.

The man with the grudge looked at His hand and then up into those smiling eyes, "Do I know You?"

The Stranger didn't answer, but instead threw an intriguing invitation before the man.

"Come," said the Stranger. "Let me show you what I do with these kinds of stones."

The two of them had jogged into a remote area beyond the town. The scent of pine filled the air. The sun was starting to crest the hillside. Morning was dawning. The two of them began to walk a narrow dirt path to the summit of a hill. There, another small path was being built with stones.

"Come follow," the Stranger said to the man with the grudge.

They walked and walked, stepping on stone after stone. Every now and then, the Stranger would bend down and touch one knowingly and a tear or two would drop onto that stone. The man with the grudge felt embarrassed by this weeping. Yet he couldn't find anything in himself to comfort the Stranger. Instead, he just followed him.

Then the Stranger with smiling eyes turned around, held out His scarred hand once again, and pointed with His other hand. "Here. This is where yours belongs."

The man stared at the empty hole surrounded by other stones so much like his. This was no easy thing being asked of him. In the seconds that transpired, he felt a fight inside of him. *Don't let go! Keep it; it's yours*, a voice seemed to say to him.

Now the Stranger was bending over the open place where the stone would lay and was weeping once again. The man knew these tears were for him. He bent down, and with shaking, sweating hands, he placed his rock-hard grudge into the shallow hole. The Stranger then pressed it down hard and pushed the dirt in around it with those now familiar scarred hands. As He did this, the Stranger whispered some kind of a prayer or benediction. The man could barely hear the words—

Child, you are worth My stone-shaped scar.

They both took a deep breath and the man with smiling eyes said once again, "Come. I want to show you something you would never have seen until now."

They walked the stone path until they reached the top of the hill where a wall and ledge began. It was made out of more grudge stones.

"Here. Let me give you a boost up." Willing to trust the Stranger now, he placed his foot into those scarred hands and allowed The Stranger to help him up to the top of the wall. Once safely on top of its ledge, the man instinctively turned around to help the Stranger up. They steadied each other and planted their feet firmly.

Then they both looked out upon an expanse of breathtaking beauty stretching far beyond what one could see with human eyes. The Stranger said, "This is what I've always wanted for you."

It was awe-inspiring and hope-filled. The man could see his tiny home from this place so high above where he'd lived with his grudge. And something began to rise inside of him—gratitude mingled with an inexplicable feeling of freedom. He turned to the Stranger, whose smiling eyes were still wet with tears, and said, "Thank you. Oh, thank you."

"This will always be here for you. Always." They both stood there a while longer, drinking it all in.

Then the Stranger with smiling eyes said, "Race you back to home?"

"You're on!" And with a new lightness, the free man—the man *without* a grudge—ran with his new Companion back home. ❖

SUITCASES

What's in your suitcase?

A story about the Cross

and letting go.

$\mathscr{S}$uitcases. He always had one with him. Sometimes two, three, even six of them at a time—suitcases—in varying sizes with varying contents. In one, the man kept a funny blue scrap of his very own baby blanket wrapped around Mr. Tiger, along with worn copies of *Robin Hood, King Arthur and the Knights of the Round Table,* and *The Adventures of Huckleberry Finn.*

One held an assortment of rare baseball cards—a Mickey Mantle rookie card, a catcher's mitt, several prized trophies, and a photo album documenting all of his athletic accomplishments.

Another suitcase held a ton of his school papers—all marked with A's. Another suitcase held mementos such as cards, letters, journals, and a book of poetry he'd started in college when he fancied himself a young Carl Sandburg.

Another held his two college degrees, countless certificates of achievement, his honor cords, frat pins, and most recent awards.

And in the smallest of all suitcases—his briefcase—there was a copy of his last big deal, signed on the dotted line and folded inside a thank you letter from his clients.

They meant everything to him, his suitcases. They kept life neat and orderly. Life made sense when he held one of those traveling bags. One look inside and his confidence swelled. These containers defined him. They reminded him. They told him he was really worth something. They were important—very important—to the man.

It was a beautiful November afternoon, the perfect California fall day: trees turning colors late, and cold but not too cold. The man had parked his car in a garage several blocks from his office so he could walk to pump up the edge he needed after lunch. He had all his suitcases with him that day. He needed all of them that day. It had been a hard one already and he knew the suitcases would help soothe him, remind him of who he really was.

The darkness of its shadow fell across the sun-drenched sidewalk before him. Suddenly, the enormous reality stared him in the face. For the first time in all of his existence, he saw what he could never quite imagine in his mind: Jesus on the cross. Jesus bleeding, beaten, stripped of most of His clothing, barely breathing, and hanging by hands and feet that had been pierced all the way through with enormous nails.

The man gripped his suitcases tightly as he looked up at Jesus. He swallowed hard. He wanted to turn and run. But on that day, he felt the presence of others there at the cross. Looking to his left he saw John with his arms wrapped around the mother of Jesus. Two other women huddled close by, quietly weeping. Others stood farther away, just watching.

Then from high up on the cross, Jesus said to the man, "What are you holding?"

"My, my suitcases, Lord," mumbled the man.

"Give them to me," said Jesus.

"But how can I give them to you? Your hands—they're bleeding. They're nailed to the cross. You're too weak to hold suitcases."

Again Jesus said it: "Give them to Me."

"I don't have a ladder, Lord. I don't know how to get them all the way up there to You."

"Put them under My cross," Jesus barely breathed the words, but the man heard them.

"Yes, Jesus. What a good idea! I can reach Him that way. If I stack up all my suitcases, I can climb up to Him and try to help."

The man quickly set to work stacking his beloved suitcases one by one. He then began to climb.

"Jesus, I'm coming. Jesus, look! I'm almost there."

But it seemed to take forever to climb the suitcases. His feet slipped off of the edges. Once, his foot got stuck in one of the handles and he thought he and his suitcases were going to topple over.

Finally, he touched Jesus' sandy, bloody feet. *Careful,* he thought. *His feet must be in such pain from that nail.*

He steadied himself on his final suitcase—the one that held his most important treasures. The height was frightening, dizzying. Barely holding onto Jesus and the cross, he could feel Jesus' chest heave to catch the next breath. He certainly didn't want to cause Him more pain, so he bore as much weight as possible on his precarious perch of suitcases.

"Jesus, I'm here. I put every suitcase under Your feet, just as You told me, and I climbed up all of them so that I can help You."

And Jesus said, "Now, give all the suitcases to me."

·"Well, Lord, I know what's in them. Just tell me what you need."

"I want the suitcases," Jesus pleaded with the man. "I want the suitcases."

"Please, Lord. I've worked hard for everything in these suitcases."

"Give them to me."

"They're all I have."

"Give them to me."

Jesus' eyes were awash with tears, and He choked as He wept for the man.

All of a sudden, the man was overcome with embarrassment. Could the others gathered below hear what was going on between them?

Then with unexpected strength Jesus said, "Just step off that last one—now."

Jesus' wounds seemed far beyond first aid, but the man tried one more excuse.

"But Jesus, I have a first aid kit in that one and my Red Cross badge and card—the very one I'm standing on right now."

"Give them to me."

"I can't." He whimpered like a little boy.

"You can. Step off."

This strange argument had started up again, but now the man was the one crying.

"I'll fall. I won't have anything left to stand on if I step off."

"Do it. Now."

"I'm so afraid. They're everything I am. What will I hold onto if I step off of this last suitcase?"

And Jesus with His unfathomable love looked at this man and said, "Me."

His warm breath and the force with which He said that one word—Me—was like a strong embrace.

The man flung his arms around Jesus' legs and kicked the suitcases away. To his amazement he didn't fall. In fact, he felt weightless and free as he watched the pile of suitcases tumble to the ground and land among all the others. Yes, there were other suitcases, thousands upon thousands of them scattered all over the ground under the cross. Why hadn't he noticed them? Where had they come from?

Holding on to Jesus was the most wonderful thing he had ever felt in all of his life. He was fastened to Jesus and the cross.

"It is finished," Jesus breathed. And the man felt all of the life drain out of the Lord's body. Thunder cracked in agreement with those last words from His mouth. Rain began to fall—a heavy rain that immediately soaked the man's clothing. But still, he clung to Him. He didn't want this to be over—this clinging to Jesus, this holding on to Him.

After what seemed like hours, he felt strong arms lifting him off the cross. And warmth. Dry sunlight warmed him. He was no longer soaking wet. It was the same November day and hour and he was standing on the same sidewalk where it had all begun. He could not see the cross. But his suitcases were scattered all over the ground, as if they'd been dropped from a great height.

His first impulse, to his surprise, was not to pick them up, but to walk away. And so he did. On that day, the man left all his suitcases at the cross. ⟡

THE GREAT KING'S LONGING

The second chapter of

"The King Who Waits."

It's only appropriate that the last story

of this collection of stories should have

everything to do with the first—

The Great King and

His love so full!

There is a King unlike any other king you've read about in history books or fairy tales. A king more wonderful than any person has ever been able to describe, more wonderful than any who ever lived among us. For this one Great King does not seek only power or rule but relationship with all of His subjects. And to those who seek Him earnestly, all the wonders and riches and treasures of the Universe are opened, all the Great King has been saving for them since the beginning of time.

And what does this Great King want in return for all of that? It's so simple, seemingly small and yet huge: just that we come to Him.

One day long ago, after many years of my own self-imposed guilt and obligation of going back and forth to the King's mansion, on one late-into-the-evening visit after a day filled with hurrying and wasting and giving and grabbing, the King told me something that changed my life. I sat down at a small table in the King's beautiful kitchen where we had shared many meals and heard, "I want you, dear child." He said it with nail-scarred hands stretched across a wooden table, His eyes smiling. "I simply want you."

In that moment our relationship was redefined forever. And my reason for going to the Mansion changed. I was wanted. And come I did. Obligation and guilt dissolved into a sea of forgetfulness as a new relationship with the Great King emerged.

Sometimes I came with so many words to share. He would lead me to one of His overstuffed chairs and we'd sit for long hours. Such a good listener, the Great King!

Sometimes I would worship and dance before Him (I'm no dancer!). Sometimes I'd present a story as a gift, or sing a song.

Sometimes I would come with filthy hands and dirty feet, making muddy tracks across the polished marble floors of His mansion. I didn't want to come when I looked like that, but those outstretched hands and those words, "I simply want you," would beckon me.

A large basin filled with warm soapy water and towels stacked high would be waiting and ready on those days. And the Great King, on bended knee, would wash me clean. It was in those times that the King would tell me how treasured I was, how dear to Him. He'd kiss my forehead and say,

"This, my Child, is where kisses really count."

Sometimes I would come with huge questions and deep concerns, and The King would pull volume after volume off the shelves of His massive library. I became the student and He was the Teacher. We'd pour over the pages for hours, sometimes late into the evening.

Other times, I'd come before the King feeling giddy and silly and other times with not a word to share. Can you imagine that—a writer without words, a storyteller without a story? But laughing and loud, silent and thinking, filthy and sad, my coming mattered much more than the state I was in. The Great King just wanted me. Me!

Time rolled on in the relationship I shared with the Great King. Complacency set in—like a familiar old sweater that wraps one up in its warmth and security. I was so cozy and content that I could subsist on memories for days. In fact, I let stale habits replace the new intimacies in our relationship. How could that be? How could I settle for feelings instead of relationship with the Great King? That was so puzzling to me. How could I let myself be satisfied with less?

Anyway, I was embarrassed after a week's absence. I tried to make amends with flowers, tea, and the books I'd borrowed. I headed to the mansion to make my apologies known. But to my surprise, the Great King opened the mansion doors before I even had a chance to knock upon them, much less apologize.

"Come with me. I want to show you something," He said excitedly.

He seemed happy to see me but insistent in His request. I'd never visited many of the other rooms in the mansion. There was no need to venture further than the ground floor for me. I loved the Library. I loved the Drawing Room, the Kitchen, and the Living Room. Those rooms were plenty for me. I knew every part of them. And that's where I always found the Great King waiting for me.

"But dear King, I have books that I've borrowed," I told Him. Anxiety rose in me. I wanted to stay in the Library today.

"Leave them on the table."

Another excuse poured out, "And I've brought some tea that I know You will love."

"We'll have it later."

"Couldn't we just stay here today?"

"No." His outstretched hand beckoned me from the first step of the staircase. "Come. Come and see what I have for you."

That familiar outstretched hand and those welcoming words brought curiosity to my heart. I took His hand and we began our ascent up the grand staircase of the Mansion.

I was in a nervous, talkative mood after such a long absence. You know that feeling. As we casually walked the first few flights, I noticed the beautiful walls were filled with pictures of His dear children. I chattered away about this subject and that subject as they caught my eye. The Great King would nod an acknowledgement or say a word or two, but not much. I seemed to be doing all the talking that day.

As we came to the landing on each floor, there were long hallways and doors that stretched out in either direction. Yet we didn't stop. Up, up, up we climbed. The walls turned from ornate wall coverings and His subjects' portraits to carefully laid stonework.

I asked the King about this change and He said, "The simplicity pleases my eye." I tried to make sense of that, but I couldn't.

I became a bit winded as the Great King picked up the pace. There was less to talk about, and I didn't have the breath for it. Silence seemed to take up the space between us. And up, up, up we climbed. Higher and higher and smaller and smaller the staircase became.

"Please, dear King," I said. "I need to rest for a second."

He stopped immediately and I stopped, gasping for air. "Ready?" He said after just a moment.

"For what?"

"More."

Frustrated I asked, "More climbing? Great King, what could possibly be way up here at the top of your Mansion that I can't get on the main floor—or on all the floors we've passed for that matter?" I sat down to punctuate my feelings. Then I became aware of my voice bouncing off the walls and the coldness of the hard stone step beneath me.

The Great King sat down beside me and wrapped His big, old robes around me. Immediately I felt warmed. We sat there quietly for a moment or two. There was stillness in that stairwell. I couldn't remember being this quiet in His presence for a long time. I laid my head on His knee, and His hand came up to rest on my back.

At that moment, my eyes caught our reflection in a huge, ornate, and gilded mirror on the stairwell wall opposite where we were seated. I looked at the Great King and me wedged between the stone wall and the balustrades of the staircase at what appeared to be almost the very top of the Mansion.

I suddenly felt very small in His presence. In fact, I looked like a small child sitting next to Him, with His endless robes enfolding me, filling the stairwell, and cascading down the steps like a flood of endless waters.

I stared into that huge mirror. His gaze rested upon me in such tenderness. What a perfect picture had been framed there. The staircase became a Throne Room and there I sat with His Majesty. I began to weep quietly, not for sadness, but for the beauty and wonder this moment contained. I beheld the unfathomable Longing Love of the Great King.

After what seemed a very long time and yet a moment, He turned toward the mirror and spoke. "Would you like to go back down? We can climb up to the very top another day. You now know that I have gifts for you that can only be reached by climbing up high in the Mansion with Me."

His smiling eyes on that phrase "climbing high" made me smile too. "Dear King, I, I think. . . ."

"Yes?" He coaxed me as a loving parent would His child.

"I want more. I want this and whatever is at the top up there."

He held out His nail-scarred hand invitingly. "Then take My hand and come with Me. We're very close." ⚜

Touch Lives with Your Story

May the story you live out today change someone. I know it can.

This announcement has been on my phone line for years. I've had people call just to write the words down. And I've had people tell me in the phone message they've left for me, "Thanks. I needed to hear that today."

I find it amazing that hearing something so simple can help someone feel better. But again, it comes back to that thing I shared with you earlier. We are forgetful people, and we need to restore our story. We forget, completely or momentarily, that we are made in God's image, and the story we are living out today matters to Him. Our story matters to those around us, too.

Whenever I tell stories, I take a moment to remind people of the power of their *own* story. Oh, I love how the stories I have told—whether fable, folktale, fairy tale, or fiction—have brought a room full of strangers together, creating the possibility of the restoration of their stories. But I want to remind my listeners of their own role as storytellers in this world—that they are a living story.

"Me, my story? Someone would want to hear my story?"

Oh yes! I have learned the power of a *true story*—the slice of life lifted out of someone's story. People listen differently to a true story, whether it is my own true story or a portion of the true story lifted from another person's life. A true story with universal meaning and value allows the listener to identify personally. This kind of story has weightiness to it. We lean in. We ask questions of our own story as we listen. We relate it to our story or the stories of those we know and love.

None of us are story-less. We carry our stories with us wherever we go in life. Some parts of my story I share only with those I trust completely. Some parts of my restored story have brought healing, because that particular part has universal meaning and value. I offer that portion out loud and on purpose to my audience. And parts of my story are in the process of restoration. I wait upon the nudge of God to share those portions, knowing they can bring hope to someone one day.

Someone needs a piece of your story to live, to laugh, to think, to be lifted up today. You're the only one who can tell it. Tell it well. Tell it out loud. Tell it on purpose.

In closing out this conversation we've been having between the stories, I would like to pray for your story and for my story:

Father,

Thank you for communicating with us in pictures, words, detailed description, dialogue . . . and in the silence. Thank you for the Story you began years and years and years ago and thank you that we have a place in this Story. You marked out our part and placed us here in your Story. That is too incredible and too big for us sometimes, Father.

Speak into the hearts and minds and souls and spirits of my readers. Come close and restore stories that have been wounded and broken and confused by what was written upon the pages of people's lives. Come close and speak in that still, small voice. Tell them they matter to You. Give them a future and a hope. Let their story be used in both big and small ways. May the story they live out today change someone. Amen.

Permissions & Use
of My Stories

"Ask, communicate, and agree.

In this way we honor one another when we use a fellow artist's work."

—Gary Bayer, my story mentor

You have my permission to take these stories and use them in classrooms, church gatherings, boardrooms, small group settings, Sunday School, Bible Studies— anywhere a group of people gather on a regular basis. Nothing would please me more than knowing that one of my stories is creating an opportunity to restore, refresh, or give a greater understanding of God.

In these particular settings, I ask that no recordings of any kind be made of my work or printed copies handed out of my stories. Please cite my authorship and direct those interested in their source to my web site or e-mail address so they can secure copies of the book and CD, as well as other audio and book products by Right-Side-Up Stories.

If you would like to take my stories into public settings for performance of any kind, you must seek my written permission for their use beforehand. We will, together, arrange for their use as would be typical for the use of a play or dramatic scene.

"Ask, communicate, and agree" seems like such an obvious way to deal with one another as fellow artists. But my friend and mentor, Gary Bayer, will tell you that this principle is more honored in the mainstream than within the church. He calls it "the holy exemption," where one feels there's no need to ask permission of a fellow believer since we're one big happy family. Actually, we dishonor one another when we do this. I want to be known as an artist who generates honor and respect, and I know you do, too. So please ask permission before using my work in public performance.

I have gained some wonderful relationships as I have shared my stories with dancers, mime artists, storytellers, actors, pastors, and other creative arts ministries. It thrills me to hear the reports of the use of my stories around the world. Please send those reports back to me. They bring such encouragement to this storyteller!

Here is my contact information:

Melea J. Brock
Right-Side-Up Stories
P.O. Box 1508
Sierra Madre, CA 91025-9508
(800)369-9230
(626) 836-3532
www.astory4u.com
astory4u@earthlink.net

For more of Melea's audio and books:

Melea J. Brock
Right-Side-Up Stories
P.O. Box 1508
Sierra Madre, CA 91025-9508
(800)369-9230
(626) 836-3532
www.astory4u.com
astory4u@earthlink.net

To order additional copies of this title call:
1-877-421-READ (7323)
or please visit our Web site at
www.winepressbooks.com

If you enjoyed this quality custom-published book,
drop by our Web site for more books and information.

www.winepressgroup.com
"Your partner in custom publishing."